Mauby's
Big Adventure

By Peter Laurie
Illustrated by H. Ann Dodson

Mauby the cat was bored. She lived on a small farm in the hills of a sunny green island in the Caribbean Sea. Shady mahogany trees grew at the front of the farm. At the back was an orchard full of mangos, coconuts, oranges, golden apples, soursops and many other fruits. A little stream flowed through the farmyard. Beside the stream was a windmill.

Mauby yawned. She looked around the farmyard. The same old chickens were pecking in the dirt. The same old pigs were playing in the mud. The same old lazy dog, Bongo, was asleep in his kennel. Out on the pasture the same silly old black-belly sheep were bleating all the time, and the same old fat cows stood chewing the cud.

Mauby was tired of it all. She was tired of catching mice. She was tired of drinking bowls of creamy milk day after day. Every morning the sun would rise above the sea like an orange ball of fire, make its way across the blue sky and sink below the green hills in the evening. Day after day, it was the same.

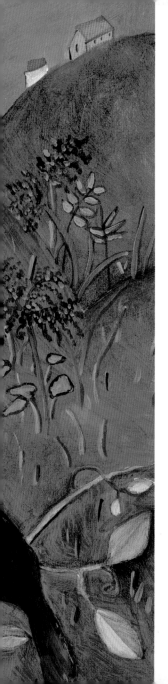

'How boring,' sighed Mauby, flicking her black and white tail restlessly. She gazed at the blue sea far away. 'Oh, how I would love to be by the sea.' And she started to dream of pirate ships and treasure hidden in caves along the water's edge. 'Now that's the life for me. Oh, to be by the sea!' she cried aloud.

'Well, why don't you just shut up and go?' A harsh voice came from on high. Mauby looked up and saw Tiki-Tak, the blackbird, sitting on a branch among the bright red flowers of a frangipani tree. Mauby hated Tiki-Tak. The blackbird had nearly pecked off Mauby's ear once for trying to catch one of her young ones.

'Why don't you mind your own business? I wasn't talking to you!' Mauby said.

'Ha, ha, ha,' chirped Tiki-Tak. 'You are just a scaredy-cat. I know you will never leave this farm.' And laughing, Tiki-Tak flew away.

Mauby made up her mind right there and then to go down to the sea. She would go the very next day. She would get away from the boredom of the farm.

Bright and early next morning, after drinking her bowl of milk, Mauby set off for the sea. She was a little afraid, to tell the truth. She had never gone more than a few yards from the farm. She gazed at the sea in the distance. It did seem a very long way away. She would have to cross many fields, a big, deep gully and a river before she could reach the seashore. Mauby jumped down from the fence and walked off across the pasture. Behind her, blackbirds in a mango tree chirped loudly.

'You'd better watch out,' Tiki-Tak's harsh voice rang out. 'There's a monster in the gully: a great big orange monster. And he's going to swallow you whole and spit out your skin and bones.' All the blackbirds shrieked with laughter.

Mauby flicked her tail proudly and went under the sweet lime hedge and out of the pasture into the open country. She saw two white egrets picking at cattle ticks in the grass. She thought she'd pounce on one and eat it for breakfast. She crawled on her belly through the grass, closer and closer. Suddenly a squeal came from a bunch of grass near her. Out of the grass came a brown animal like a large rat. It stood on its hind legs, its long bushy tail sticking straight up in the air. Its sharp teeth were bared. It was Sly One, the mongoose.

'What are you doing here?' he hissed angrily. 'This is my land. Get off!' Sly One's little black eyes gleamed fiercely.

Mauby had heard a lot about Sly One, although she had never met him. Everyone on the farm hated him. He sneaked into the chicken pens and stole eggs and sometimes little chicks. Bongo was his enemy and Mr Hunte, the farmer, fired his shotgun at him whenever he saw him. But Sly One was so clever no one ever caught him.

'I'm sorry,' said Mauby. 'I didn't know this was your land. I'm from the farm and I was making my way to the sea. I thought I'd have an egret for breakfast.'

'Well you can't. I'm the only one who can hunt on this land. Besides, I know who you are. Why do you want to go to the sea?'

'Because I'm bored,' replied Mauby.

'What a stupid reason. I advise you to go back home. There are many dangers out here in the wild.'

'Thank you,' said Mauby crossly. 'But I think I'll be on my way.'

'Well,' said Sly One, rubbing his chin with his paw, 'since you are so set on going, I'll help you by showing you the way. But don't say I didn't warn you.' And Sly One ran off through the grass.

Mauby hurried to catch up. She didn't trust Sly One, but she did need all the help she could get to find her way to the sea. They crossed a few pastures and squeezed through hedges full of thorns. Sly One found holes that were just the right size for him but a little too tight for Mauby. She left patches of her fur stuck in the hedges. Then they went through several fields of sugar cane. The sharp leaves of the canes scratched Mauby's face. She was getting hot, tired and thirsty as the sun rose in the bright blue sky. She longed for a bowl of delicious milk and the cool shade of the mango tree by the water trough in the farmyard.

'Here's the first tricky part,' said Sly One. 'We have to cross a main road. There's really nothing to it if you have **instincts** – the instincts of the wild.' The mongoose looked at the cat. 'Of course, if you don't have instincts you might get run over by a great big truck or tractor. Do you have instincts?'

'Of course I have instincts. I am a cat,' said Mauby proudly. But she did not feel quite as sure as she sounded.

'Okay, listen to me,' said Sly One. 'I'll cross the road first and then let you know when it's safe to cross. I'll stick my tail up. When I bring it down you run like mad. Don't look right or left but straight ahead.' This sounded odd to Mauby, whose mother had always told her to look right and left before crossing any path.

Sly One waited and listened. Then he darted across the road. Once on the other side he sat between two bunches of khus-khus grass. He raised his tail. Mauby watched him closely, ready to run. She could hear a faint humming in the distance. The humming got louder and louder. Suddenly Sly One's tail came down. Mauby leaped into the road. She was almost in the middle of the road when she heard a roar and a screech. A big truck laden with sugar canes was almost upon her. She slid to a stop just as the enormous front wheel passed her. Frightened, she dashed beneath the truck. She almost got run over by a back wheel. She reached the other side of the road. She didn't stop running until she was halfway across the pasture.

14

Her heart was beating madly and she was puffing and panting. Sly One caught up with her.

'Tst, tst, tst.' Sly One shook his head. 'No instincts! None at all. I was right. A sad case you are.'

Mauby was angry. 'You pulled down your tail just as the truck was passing. You almost got me killed!' shouted Mauby.

'Don't be silly,' replied Sly One. 'You got it wrong. You have to have instincts. Anyway it's almost midday. Time we stopped for a little snack and a nap.'

They stopped in the shade of a guava tree.

'Just a second. I'll be back with some food.' And the mongoose slipped away into the hedge.

Mauby lay on her stomach and licked her fur. It was full of burrs and thorns and thistles. She felt hungry, thirsty and hot and very unhappy. Sly One came back in a few minutes with a couple of birds' eggs.

'Here,' he said, 'one for you. It's nice and rotten.'

'I don't eat eggs!' said Mauby angrily. And she curled up and went to sleep, dreaming of buckets of creamy milk.

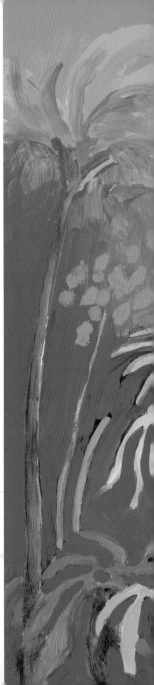

They set off again in the afternoon. A cool breeze was blowing off the sea. Mauby looked back up the long hill they had come down. In the distance she could see the roof of the farmhouse among the trees and the windmill turning. She wanted to turn back, but was too proud to do so. She would not quit.

They came to another farm. They could hear dogs barking. They went around it, crawling along a muddy ditch. They crossed several more pastures and cane fields. They came to the gully just as the evening shadows began to grow long. It was deep and very long. It would take a long time to go around it.

'This is where I leave you; my land stops here,' said Sly One.

Mauby was afraid. 'But how do I get across?' She remembered what Tiki-Tak had said about the great orange monster in the gully.

'Well,' said Sly One, 'you can try to go around it. But you would have to walk for several hours. Besides, you would have to pass through a village where the stray dogs eat cats like you. Or you can go over the gully. I'll show you my secret way, if you like. But whatever you do, do **not** go into the gully. For sure, you won't come out alive. Sheep and cows that have fallen into the gully have never come out. Not even their bones have been found. And do you know why?'

He paused and smiled wickedly at Mauby. She was quite frightened but tried hard not to show it.

'Because there is an enormous macajuel snake that lives in that gully. He is over twenty feet long. His jaws open so wide they can swallow a cow. That's after he has wrapped himself around it and squeezed it as flat as a bake.'

Mauby was too terrified to say anything.

'Luckily for you,' went on Sly One, ' I know a secret way over the gully. I'll show you because I'm such a nice mongoose. Follow me.' And he raced off along the edge of the gully. Mauby followed him as best she could.

They soon came to a place where the gully was no more than thirty feet wide. The sides of the gully were steep. They were covered in vines and bush. Mauby could see the tops of trees growing out of the gully. Tall bamboo grew nearby. The mongoose led Mauby through the bamboo right to the edge of the gully. A long pole of bamboo had fallen across it. Its slender top rested on the other side.

'This is it,' said Sly One, pointing with his paw at the bamboo pole. 'My secret bridge across the gully.'

Mauby's heart sank. There was no way she could walk across that pole. She could not stand heights. Once she had got stuck up a tree and one of the farm workers had had to climb up and rescue her.

'You'd better get a move on,' said Sly One. 'If you get caught in the dark, you'll never get across.' But Mauby just stood staring at the long, thin pole that stretched across the deep dark gully. She felt quite sick.

'C'mon!' Sly One said to her impatiently. But she did not move. 'Ah, well, let me show you how.' The mongoose scurried across the pole to the other side and then ran back again. 'You see. It's easy. There's nothing to it.'

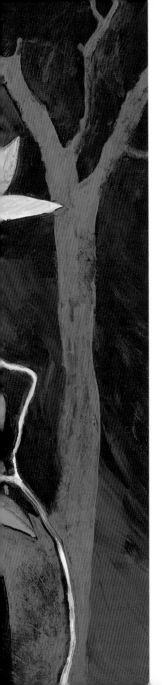

Mauby stepped on to the bamboo pole. At this end it was thick, and it wasn't too hard for her to walk the first few feet. Then the pole began to get thinner and thinner. She tried to grip the pole with her claws as she walked along it. She used her tail to help her balance. She kept telling herself not to look down. Just as she was past the halfway point the pole began to wobble. Mauby was ten times as heavy as the mongoose. She tried to turn around but this only made the pole wobble more. Her back feet slipped off and she clung in fear to the shaking pole with her front feet. Then the pole spun and she lost her grip. As she fell she heard Sly One shouting 'No instincts, no instincts!' and 'Watch out for the orange monster!'

Mauby crashed into the top branches of a tree. She went on falling. She kept saying to herself: a cat always lands on its feet; a cat has nine lives. She hit a large branch. It knocked the breath out of her. But she was able to cling on. She slid down the branch until she came to a fork. She stopped.

She had fallen about forty feet. A cat must have nine lives! She was safe! She looked around her. All she could see were leaves and branches. Above her she could see bits of the sky through the leaves. But when she looked down it was dark. How was she going to get out? She couldn't go up. She would have to go down and try to find a way up the side of the gully. She must be at least eighty feet above the ground. Down below it was now pitch black. Then she remembered that she could see in the dark. Didn't she hunt mice at night on the farm? Besides it was full moon. The moon would shortly be coming up over the sea. By its light she would be able to find her way out of this gully. She felt a lot better now so she sat quietly in the tree fork and waited for the moon to come up.

Mauby soon heard the sounds of the night all around her. Frogs were whistling and croaking, crickets were chirping, monkeys were chattering and bats were squeaking. She was glad to hear these familiar sounds. The moon rose and cast its pale light into the gully.

Then Mauby heard a strange sound. It was a soft, hissing, slithering noise. She pricked up her ears and listened closely. The sound seemed to be coming from below her. She peered through the leaves. She saw nothing but a thick, long branch that moved gently in the wind. But there **was** no wind. The night was still. The hissing and slithering noise came closer. The branch was now twisting about as it reached up towards her from below.

At that moment Mauby remembered the orange monster: the macajuel snake that was over twenty feet long and gobbled up its prey whole. Every hair on her body stood on end and her ears were flat against her head. Suddenly the horrible orange head of a gigantic snake with shining red eyes appeared right below her. It slowly opened its huge mouth, its long, forked tongue flicking out at her. Giving a loud shriek Mauby leaped with all her strength away from the snake into the dark. Her four legs spread wide, she fell through the branches and leaves, tumbling and turning until she crashed into a bush and landed on the ground on her feet.

Still screaming at the top of her voice, she took off.
She didn't know where she was going. For the first time
in her life she simply followed her instincts. Running around
bushes and leaping over logs and stones she raced along
the bottom of the gully. And then, just as she was about to
fall into a deep pit in the ground, she turned and dashed up
the side of the gully to the top. She didn't stop, but ran
across the fields in the moonlight until she came to the
bank of a river where she flung herself down.

Mauby had never been so terrified in her life. She shook with fear as she remembered the shining red eyes of the macajuel.

'Excuse me. You're blocking my hole.'

Mauby nearly jumped out of her skin at the sound of a voice right behind her. Leaping up and turning, Mauby saw a large reddish brown crab with two fearsome claws looking at her.

31

'Thank you,' said the crab. 'Sorry to have frightened you, but you were lying on top of my hole.' The crab, seeing that Mauby still looked afraid, said with a laugh, 'Oh don't be afraid, I don't eat cats. By the way, my name is Clipper. What's yours?'

'Mauby,' said the cat, keeping her eyes on the crab's claws.

'Relax,' said Clipper. 'Would you like to share a fish with me? I had just caught it in the river and was taking it to my hole to eat before I set off on my walk.' A fish was just what Mauby wanted, so she took half of the fish that Clipper held out to her in her claw. It was delicious and Mauby soon ate every scrap of it.

'So tell me, what is a cat doing out by the river in the middle of the night?'

Mauby told Clipper all that had happened to her from the time she had left the farm, ending with her meeting with the macajuel in the gully.

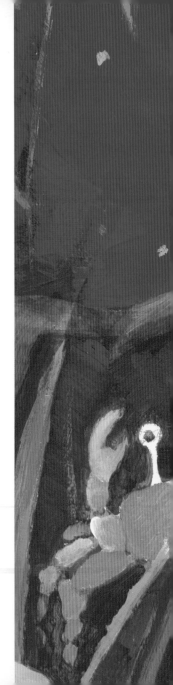

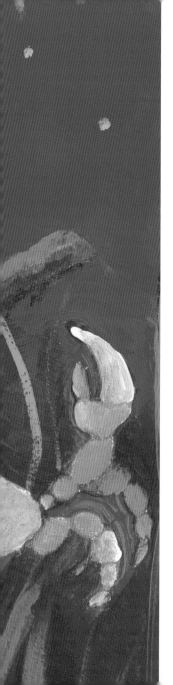

'You're really lucky,' said Clipper. 'Most animals who meet that monster don't live to tell about it. Maybe cats do have nine lives.' She chuckled. 'Well, you are also lucky you met me, because I'm off to the sea myself, and if you like you can come with me. I know the way very well.'

'Why are you going to the sea?' Mauby asked.

'To lay my eggs. Every full moon we female land crabs go down to the sea to lay our eggs,' replied Clipper.

'But why don't you just lay them here in the river?'
Mauby asked.

'Because Nature made it that way. Our eggs will only hatch in the sea,' said Clipper.

'Then why don't you live on the seashore?' Mauby asked.

'My, you are a curious cat,' said Clipper. 'Nature meant us to live by a river or a swamp.'

Mauby thought it rather silly to have to spend your life walking two miles back and forth every month just to lay eggs. But she didn't say so because she didn't want to be unkind to her new friend. She was glad, however, that she wasn't a crab.

'Okay, let's go,' said Clipper. 'If we hurry we can get there by dawn. I will lay my eggs just at the water's edge. Then I'll hide among the rocks until night comes and come back up the river. We only move by night. It's safer. And we stay close to the river so if there is any danger we scurry down a hole. I'm afraid you wouldn't be able to get down a crab hole. But then you can run a lot faster than I can.' Mauby didn't say what she was thinking: she would rather die than crawl into a dark, muddy, crab hole.

Clipper and Mauby set off, following the river down to the sea. They walked along the sloping bank of the river. The bank was dotted with crab holes. They saw other crabs making their way down to the sea.

The full moon shone brightly in the sky. The sea below sparkled. The sand on the shore was dazzling white.

'Have you ever found any treasure by the seashore?' asked Mauby.

'Treasure?!' snorted Clipper. 'All you ever find down there are plastic bottles, plastic cups and plastic bags. Humans are terrible creatures. They dump all their garbage in the sea. They have also made the river filthy. Not much treasure, my dear. I'm afraid things aren't what you think they are out here. You're much better off on the farm, believe me!' said Clipper sadly. 'What's more,' Clipper continued, 'there's a horrible fish who lurks just at the mouth of the river to see what garbage the river will wash into the sea. It's a large tiger shark with great big teeth. So you just make sure you stay out of the water or he'll have you for breakfast.'

Mauby shuddered.

Mauby walked the rest of the way in silence. She thought of life back on the farm. The cows being milked early in the morning, the black-belly sheep let out to graze on the pasture, the eggs picked up and the rabbits fed. She thought of teasing Bongo; of chasing lizards; of catching mice and of quarrelling with Tiki-Tak. She thought of lovely afternoon naps in the shade of the mango tree and bowls of delicious creamy milk. It all seemed so far away now.

It was getting light as they reached the beach. The sun was just beginning to rise above the sea. Clipper said she would go into the water and lay her eggs in a pool among the rocks. She warned Mauby to stay far from the sea since the waves were big and strong, and the shark usually waited just beyond the waves that crashed on the beach.

Mauby sat on a rock on the beach and watched Clipper crawl down to the water. A wave broke on the shore and the surf swept up the beach. The white foam covered Clipper and took her with it as it ran back into the sea.

Mauby became worried. Her new friend was being swept out into the ocean. She remembered what Clipper had said about the shark, but she must rescue her friend. Mauby raced across the sand to the water. She reached the edge of the water but couldn't see Clipper anywhere. She stood up on her hind legs and looked around her. Nothing. Clipper was gone.

Suddenly a huge wave rose over Mauby. She turned and tried to run back up the beach. Her paws sank into the soft sand. The wave broke over her, smashing her into the sand. She was rolled over and over and then the wave started to go back out and drag her with it.

As she tried to get a grip on the sand she looked over her shoulder and saw another wave towering above her. And in the centre of the wave she saw a grey face with two big eyes and a wide mouth full of sharp white teeth. It was the tiger shark! He was waiting for her as the water sucked her into the oncoming wave. His fierce jaws opened wide.

Just as she was giving up all hope, a hand grabbed her firmly by the scruff of the neck and pulled her out of the water. She coughed and spat out sand and water.

'My goodness, Mauby, what on earth are you doing here? You almost drowned!'

This was the sweetest sound Mauby had ever heard in her life: the voice of Farmer Hunte. He cuddled her safely in his strong arms. Farmer Hunte walked up the beach with her, picked up a towel and rubbed her down.

'Lucky for you I came to the beach to get some sand to fix the pig pen,' said the farmer. 'But what are you doing so far away from home?' Farmer Hunte gently stroked her head. 'Anyway, I'm sure you've learned your lesson. We'd better get you back home.'

Farmer Hunte carried her to his jeep parked on the road beside the beach. Mauby saw a crab scuttle out of the water and head for some rocks on the beach by the mouth of the river. Clipper was safe!

On the ride home Mauby lay curled up on the towel in the front seat next to Farmer Hunte. The rocking of the jeep and the excitement of her journey made her feel very tired. She began to nod off. She was so looking forward to seeing the farm and the cows and the sheep and the chickens and the pigs and Bongo and Tiki-Tak and… She was soon fast asleep.

Mauby would never be bored again.

48

First published 2000 by
MACMILLAN EDUCATION LTD
London and Oxford
Companies and representatives throughout the world

ISBN 0-333-77404-3

10 9 8 7 6 5 4 3 2 1
09 08 07 06 05 04 03 02 01 00

This book is printed on paper suitable for recycling and
made from fully managed and sustained forest sources.

Printed in Hong Kong

A catalogue record of this book is available from the
British Library.

Illustrated by H. Ann Dodson
Designed by Alex Tucker Holbrook Design (Oxford) Limited
Colour Separation by Tenon & Polert Colour Scanning Ltd.